This book belongs to:

_____

_____

A TREASURY OF CHRISTMAS STORIES AND SONGS

This edition published by Parragon Books Ltd in 2016
and distributed by

Parragon Inc.
440 Park Avenue South, 13th Floor
New York, NY 10016
www.parragon.com

ISBN 978-1-4748-6719-1

Printed in China

A TREASURY OF
CHRISTMAS
STORIES AND SONGS

PaRragon

Bath · New York · Cologne · Melbourne · Delhi
Hong Kong · Shenzhen · Singapore

Contents

The First Christmas

Long ago in a place called Nazareth there lived a girl named Mary. She was engaged to be married to a carpenter named Joseph, and she would daydream about their wedding as she went about her chores.

One day, Mary noticed a stranger smiling at her. She knew at once that he was an angel.

"My name is Gabriel," he said. "I have brought you a message from God."

Mary was too amazed to speak.

"God has chosen you to do something special for him," continued Gabriel. "Soon, you will have a baby, and you are to name him Jesus. He will be God's own son."

Mary was happy to do as God had asked, but Joseph felt upset because he knew he wasn't the father of the baby. He prayed to God for help.

"What should I do?" he asked. "I love Mary, but I don't know if I should still marry her."

God heard his prayers. That night, an angel visited Joseph in a dream.

"Do not worry," he told Joseph. "This baby will become a king and save his people."

"I will trust in God," Joseph decided the next morning.

So Mary and Joseph were married and they waited patiently for the baby to arrive.

Soon after the wedding, the Emperor of Rome, who ruled over the land where Mary and Joseph lived, sent out orders through his messengers.

"Everyone must travel to their place of birth to be counted," said the messengers.

Joseph had been born in Bethlehem, a long way away.

Joseph packed enough food and water for the journey, and Mary made a bundle of blankets and clothes for when the baby arrived. They said their goodbyes to friends and family and set out for Bethlehem.

The journey to Bethlehem took many days.

It was late at night when they finally arrived, and Mary was very tired.

"Let's find a place to stay for the night," said Joseph. But every inn they tried was full.

When they arrived at the last inn in town, the owner shook his head.

"There is no room at the inn," he said. "Everyone has come to Bethlehem to obey the Emperor's order."

"What can we do?" asked Mary. "My baby is coming very soon."

"Come," said the man kindly. "I have a place that might do."

16

The innkeeper led them to
a stable behind the house. It was
filled with animals and the floor
was covered with fresh straw.

"This is warm and safe,"
said Mary. "Thank you for
your kindness."

That night, Mary gave birth
to a little boy.

Joseph lined a feeding
trough with straw to make a soft
bed. Mary wrapped the baby
in a blanket and laid him down
gently in the manger.

"We'll name you Jesus, like
the angel said," whispered Mary.

Nearby, some shepherds were watching over their sheep on a hillside. Suddenly, there was a dazzling brightness all around them.

"What's happening?" they cried, as angels appeared.

"Don't be afraid," said one. "I have wonderful news. The son of God has been born in Bethlehem. He is the king that God promised."

The light faded and the angels were gone. The shepherds looked at each other in wonder.

"We must go to Bethlehem and see the baby king," they agreed.

The shepherds walked through the quiet streets until they heard a baby's cry and found the stable.

"We have come to visit the new king," they said. "God sent an angel to give us the news."

"You are all welcome," said Joseph.

"We are poor," said the shepherds as they knelt by the manger. "We have nothing to give the baby but our love."

"That is the best gift in the world," said Mary.

Soon, it was time for the shepherds to return to their sheep. They told everyone they met about the new king.

In a far-off country, three wise men noticed a new star in the sky. They knew that this meant something special.

"It is shining because a new king has been born," said one.

"Perhaps the star will lead us to him," said the second.

"Let's take some gifts and go and worship this king," said the third.

The wise men set off for the city of Jerusalem.

After travelling for many nights, the wise men arrived at the palace. They were sure they would find the new king there. They were taken to the ruler, King Herod.

"We have come to worship the new king," they said.

King Herod was worried. He wanted to be the only king in the land.

"Who is this new king they speak of?" he whispered to his advisor.

"A prophet once said that a new king would be born in Bethlehem," the advisor said.

King Herod decided he must stop the baby taking his throne.

"I want to worship the new king too," he lied. "Go to Bethlehem, then return here and tell me where I can find him."

The wise men traveled to Bethlehem, where the star led them to baby Jesus.

"We have come to see the new king," said the wise men.

Mary welcomed them in, and they knelt to give Jesus their gifts.

"Here is precious gold," said the first.

"I have brought sweet-smelling frankincense," said the second.

"And this is myrrh, a healing oil," said the third.

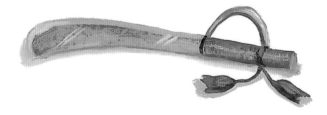

That night the wise men camped outside Bethlehem.

While they slept, God visited each of them in a dream. He warned them not to return to King Herod.

In the morning, the wise men agreed to go straight home.

King Herod was furious when he learned that the wise men had disobeyed him.

"I am the only king!" he roared. "I will not let a baby take my throne!"

God sent an angel to warn Joseph that Herod was planning to harm Jesus.

"You must leave Bethlehem at once," said the angel. "Escape to Egypt, where you will be safe."

Joseph woke Mary, and they quickly loaded their belongings onto the donkey. Carrying Jesus, they set off into the night.

Jesus was safe in Egypt, but Mary and Joseph missed Nazareth.

A few years passed peacefully. One night, God sent an angel to speak to Joseph in a dream.

"King Herod has died," said the angel. "It is safe for you to return home."

Joseph and Mary packed their belongings and set off once more. When they arrived, they were overjoyed to be back in their hometown at last.

Joseph held Jesus as he stood in the doorway of their little house.

"This is Nazareth, the town where you will grow up," he said with a smile. "Welcome home, Jesus!"

Hark! The Herald Angels Sing

Hark! The herald angels sing,
"Glory to the newborn king."
Peace on earth and mercy mild,
God and sinners reconciled.
Joyful, all you nations rise,
Join the triumph of the skies.
With the angelic hosts proclaim,
"Christ is born in Bethlehem."
Hark! The herald angels sing,
"Glory to the newborn king."

O Christmas Tree

O Christmas Tree, O Christmas tree,
How lovely are your branches!
Not only green when summer's here,
But in the coldest time of year.
O Christmas Tree, O Christmas tree,
How lovely are your branches!

The Nutcracker

It was Christmas Eve and the snow was gently falling. Clara and her brother Fritz were very excited. That night, there would be a magnificent party with music and dancing, as well as lots of fantastic presents!

Fritz was busy with his toy soldiers, lining them up and giving them their orders.

Clara put the finishing touches to their enormous tree. She hung shining ornaments and candy canes tied with bows from the branches.

"This is my favorite part," Clara said to her brother as she lifted up a beautiful fairy with delicate wings and a sugarplum-colored dress.

At last, it was time for
the party to begin.

"The guests are arriving!"
cried Clara, peeping out of her
bedroom window.

Fritz came running over to see
who was crunching through the snow.

"Can you see Godfather
Drosselmeyer?" asked Clara.

"Yes, there he is waving!"
cried Fritz. "Come on!"

Their godfather was a famous
toymaker. He made the most magical
toys in the whole city. Clara and Fritz
could hardly wait to see what he had
brought for them.

Godfather Drosselmeyer hugged the children at the door, and with a flourish, he produced two gifts.

Fritz eagerly unwrapped a mechanical jawbreaker machine. For Clara, there was a wooden nutcracker in the shape of a soldier.

"Take good care of him," said Godfather Drosselmeyer. "He is very special."

"I love him," Clara whispered. "Thank you."

"But he's a soldier," said Fritz. "He should be mine."

"You can't have him!" cried Clara.

Fritz tried to snatch the Nutcracker away from her. He pulled and Clara tugged, and then ...

CRACK!

The Nutcracker's leg snapped off!

Clara cradled the Nutcracker in her arms and wept.

"Don't cry, Clara," said her godfather gently. "This soldier has been wounded, but I can soon fix him."

Godfather Drosselmeyer pulled a little tool pouch from his pocket and quickly mended the Nutcracker, so that he looked as good as new.

"Oh, thank you," said Clara, drying her eyes. "I'll never let anyone hurt him again."

Everyone was dancing now and the house was filled with music and laughter. Clara placed the Nutcracker carefully under the Christmas tree and went to join the party.

Finally, the last dance was danced, and the guests said their goodbyes. The family went to bed, and the house was dark and quiet.

Bong!

Clara awoke to hear the last bong of the clock striking midnight.

"Oh no!" she thought. "I left the Nutcracker all alone under the tree."

Clara tiptoed downstairs and crept under the Christmas tree, holding the Nutcracker protectively.

Suddenly, the tree started to
grow. Taller and taller! Or was it
just that Clara was shrinking?
"What's happening?" she cried.

"Don't be afraid," said a kind voice suddenly. Clara turned around. Her Nutcracker had come alive! Behind him, Fritz's soldiers were sitting up in their toy box, and Clara's dolls were gazing around.

Before Clara could speak, she heard a scurrying sound, and from every nook and cranny, an army of mice poured into the room! They were led by a giant Mouse King with a golden crown.

"ATTACK!" he squealed.

"Who will fight with me?" cried the Nutcracker. The soldiers marched boldly out of the toy box.

"TO BATTLE!" ordered the Nutcracker.
The soldiers shouted and cheered, and the
mice squealed and squeaked.

Suddenly, Clara saw the Mouse King spring toward her beloved Nutcracker, baring his teeth.

"No!' cried Clara. She snatched off her slipper and hurled it at the Mouse King. He fell to the ground with a cry, and his crown tumbled from his head.

With their leader defeated, the mice scurried away in fear. The battle was won!

The Nutcracker picked up Clara's
slipper and placed it on her foot. She
gasped—the Nutcracker had been
transformed into a handsome prince!

"I owe you my life, Princess Clara," he said.
"You broke the spell that was put on me long
ago by a wicked Mouse Queen."

"I'm glad that you're safe," said Clara.
"But you are mistaken—I'm not a princess."

"Are you sure?" asked the prince.

Clara looked down and saw that she was
wearing a glittering gown and satin shoes!

"Come," said the prince. "I am going to
take you on a wonderful adventure."

The sleigh landed beside a rose-colored lake and changed into a seachariot pulled by dolphins. Swans swam beside them, and shimmering fish leapt out of the water.

On the far side of the lake was a magnificent marzipan palace. A fairy with delicate wings was waving to them from the gate.

"Look," said the prince. "It's the Sugarplum Fairy!"

"Prince Nutcracker!" cried the fairy. "You are home at last."

"This is Princess Clara," said the Prince, as they stepped ashore. "She saved my life and broke the Mouse Queen's spell."

The Sugarplum Fairy hugged Clara.

"Come and join the celebrations!" she said.

Inside the palace, Clara and the prince
feasted on delicious cakes and sweets.

They watched in wonder as dancers
from every corner of the world whirled
around the room.

Then it was the Sugarplum Fairy's turn. Clara had never seen such dancing! She twirled and twirled, until all Clara could see was the blur of her plum-colored dress.

Clara's eyelids began to droop. Her adventures had made her tired. The sound of the music became fainter and fainter ....

When Clara woke up on Christmas morning, she found herself curled up under the Christmas tree next to the Nutcracker. Toys were strewn across the floor, and her parents were standing over her.

"What have you been doing?" asked her father.

"Oh, I've had the most wonderful adventure," said Clara.

She told her parents all about the Mouse King, The Nutcracker Prince, and the Kingdom of Sweets.

"It was just a dream, darling," said her mother.

Clara gazed up at the sugarplum-colored fairy on top of the tree. Then she looked at the wooden Nutcracker in her hands.

"Perhaps it was," she said.

Suddenly, Clara noticed something glinting on the carpet, and a smile spread across her face. It was a tiny golden crown!

"Merry Christmas, Prince
Nutcracker," she whispered.

Away in a Manger

Away in a manger, no crib for a bed,
The little Lord Jesus laid down His sweet head.
The stars in the bright sky looked down where He lay,
The little Lord Jesus asleep on the hay.

The cattle are lowing, the baby awakes,
But Little Lord Jesus, no crying he makes.
I love Thee, Lord Jesus; look down from the sky,
And stay by my side until morning is nigh.

Be near me, Lord Jesus, I ask Thee to stay
Close by me forever, and love me, I pray.
Bless all the dear children in Thy tender care,
And fit us for heaven, to live with Thee there.

We Wish You
a Merry Christmas

We wish you a Merry Christmas,
We wish you a Merry Christmas,
We wish you a Merry Christmas,
And a Happy New Year!

Good tidings we bring
To you and your kin;
We wish you a Merry Christmas,
And a Happy New Year!

The Fir Tree

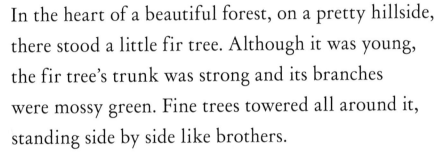

In the heart of a beautiful forest, on a pretty hillside, there stood a little fir tree. Although it was young, the fir tree's trunk was strong and its branches were mossy green. Fine trees towered all around it, standing side by side like brothers.

Every afternoon, children would run in and out of the woods, picking wild strawberries. The hillside echoed with the sound of their laughter and songs.

Days like these should have made the fir tree feel contented, but instead, all the fir tree could think about was the day when it would be as big and strong as the trees standing beside it.

When summer passed to winter, flurries of snowflakes whirled all around. But the fir tree found no joy in the glittering carpet of snow that appeared.

Even when a robin redbreast sat on the tree's branches and began a cheery song, its spirits could not be lifted.

"Be quiet," grumbled the fir tree. "Perch somewhere else."

The fir tree had no time for songbirds. It was too busy imagining itself reaching up to the sky far above. Every time it looked up at the grown-up trees, the fir tree would give another little sigh.

"What a feeling it must be to sway back and forth like they do," it would think. "How much longer until it's my turn to be big and strong?"

Year by year, the fir tree kept growing, and it began to notice new things.

Every year, after the first flurry of snowflakes, the woodcutters rode into the forest. At this time of year, they ignored the giants of the hillside—they chopped down the smaller, younger trees instead.

"Why have those trees been chosen?" wondered the fir tree.

This time, instead of stripping off their branches, the men carefully laid the felled trees on a cart, and took them away.

"What is happening?" the fir tree demanded.

Some sparrows told the fir tree what they had seen in the town, at the end of the forest trail.

"It's Christmas-time," they chirped. "Those trees will each be placed in a grand house and covered with beautiful decorations. We see them every year!"

From that moment on, the fir tree had a new ambition—to be a glorious Christmas tree!

"If only Christmas would come right now," it sighed. The fir tree could think of nothing else.

Winter thawed into spring and spring bloomed into summer, but the fir tree barely noticed. As the forest blossomed, the fir tree also stretched and grew. It was now both tall and handsome.

Walkers, hunters, and couples would all stop beside its branches.

"Look at this one," they would say, gazing at its perfect shape and glistening evergreen needles. "What a beauty!"

When Christmas came around the next year, the fir tree was the very first tree to be cut down and laid on the back of the woodcutter's cart.

Suddenly, it was sad to be leaving the forest.

"Stay calm," the fir tree told itself firmly. "Think about that warm drawing room. Think about those twinkling decorations!"

More and more trees were put on the cart. There was barely any room to breathe! Then the horse began to trot back down the forest track, pulling the cart behind it. Finally, the cart stopped in a cobbled yard peppered with snow.

"This must be the town," decided the fir tree, remembering the sparrows and their stories. "But where are the decorations?"

All the trees were unpacked from the cart and
lined up side by side against a brick wall.

"What will become of me now?" wondered the
fir tree, as a man stopped to look them up and down.

"Yes—that's the tree for us!" he nodded, when he
got to the fir tree.

The man carried the fir tree across the yard, into
a fine building.

Soon the tree found itself in a drawing room filled with oil paintings, sofas, and a grand piano. A small crowd of children watched excitedly.

The fir tree was placed in a tub filled with sand, then a jolly green cloth was tied around the base.

"Now it feels like Christmas," smiled a young lady carrying a wooden box. When she lifted the lid, the children gasped. Inside, there were velvet ribbons, glass baubles, striped candy canes, and fir cones painted silver and gold.

"Gather around," said the lady, "and join in, everyone!"

The boys and girls laughed and sang carols
as they hung up the pretty trinkets. When they'd
finished, a butler in a smart jacket placed a gold star
at the top. The fir tree was transformed. It had never
looked so splendid.

"It's lovely!" smiled a little girl with rosy cheeks.

The tree listened as the butler knelt down to
whisper in her ear.

"You wait until tonight," he said with a smile.
"Tonight, this tree will shine from top to bottom!"

The fir tree was filled with wonder. It could
hardly wait for the night to arrive!

Soon the butler and his servants began to light up the decorations. Reflections on the glass baubles sent flecks of light spinning across the ceiling.

"It's the most beautiful thing I have ever seen!" declared the little girl with rosy cheeks.

The children skipped around the fir tree, pointing at the sparkling decorations. Their stories, games, and singing lasted for hours.

Just before bedtime, a man clapped his hands.

"You've been very patient," he smiled. "Now it's time to take a trinket from the tree. Merry Christmas, everyone!"

The children jostled around the fir tree, racing to pull presents and treats off its branches.

"I hope they stop soon," thought the fir tree. "Or my branches will be bare!"

When the children had gone to bed, there was barely a present or a treat left on the tree. It felt dried out and thin.

"Never mind," the fir tree said, trying to comfort itself. "You can do it all again tomorrow!"

The fir tree dreamed all night about the fun it was going to have at the next party.

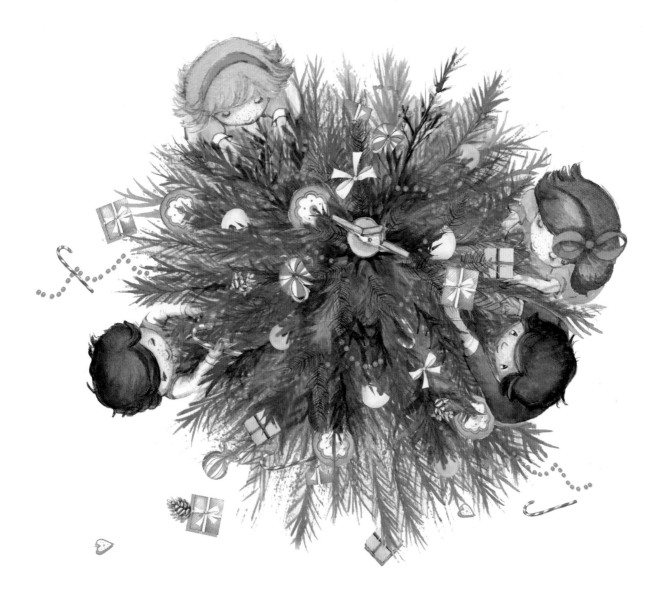

In the morning, the fir tree watched a maid open the shutters in the drawing room. Morning sunlight streamed in through the windows.

"At last!" exclaimed the fir tree. It stood as straight as it could, waiting for more presents and treats to be placed on its boughs.

Instead, the maid slowly pulled the remaining ornaments off it. The fir tree winced as each one was dusted off and packed away into a box.

"What is the meaning of this?" the fir tree asked.

Then the butler took down the tree, dragged it into the attic, and locked the door.

After a while, the fir tree began to wonder if it had been forgotten.

"The ground is hard at this time of year," it thought to itself. "They must be waiting until the spring comes before they plant me again. Yes, that must be it! How thoughtful ..."

The fir tree clung to this hope as the days passed.

In those quiet moments, it remembered its time in the forest. It wondered if it would ever see the robin redbreast again or hear its merry song.

One day, a nest of mice broke the lonely silence of the attic.

"Hello, hello!" squeaked one. "Where do you come from, old fir tree?"

The fir tree bristled. "I come from the most beautiful place—and I am hardly old," it retorted.

A mouse twitched its whiskers inquisitively. "Tell us about this beautiful place," it said.

The fir tree told the mice about the hillside where it had grown up. It explained how there were big, beautiful trees as far as the eye could see.

"How lucky you have been!" gasped the mouse.

"That isn't all," agreed the fir tree. "I have stood in the best room of this very house, with a light shining on every branch!"

The mice squeaked in awe.

Each day, the mice listened patiently to every detail of the fir tree's magical evening in the drawing room. The fir tree delighted in telling the tale over and over.

"That was such a merry time," it would say wistfully at the end. "The happiest night of my life."

The visitors all agreed that the fir tree had been very lucky indeed.

After a while however, even the curious mice had heard enough. By the time spring arrived, the fir tree was alone once again.

One fine morning, the attic door
rattled open.

"At last!" cried the fir tree.
"Now I can get back outside and start
growing again!"

The fir tree was carried out into the
yard where it had stood months before.

Outside, the sun glittered and the
cool air danced through its branches.
The fir tree wondered where it was
going to be planted.

But a different fate awaited the fir tree. The maid tossed it into a heap of nettles in the corner of the yard, then dashed off.

"This can't be right!" gasped the fir tree. "I still have lots of growing to do!"

As the fir tree lay on its side, it noticed that its lovely evergreen hue had faded into a dull brown.

"If only I had enjoyed my time on the hillside instead of wasting it," sighed the fir tree.

With that, a gardener appeared. The fir tree was chopped into pieces, thrown into the kitchen stove, and burned.

Yet, as the wood crackled and popped, the fir tree saw things clearly for the first time. It remembered the robin and the scent of the forest. It gave thanks for the beauty it had seen in its life.

Soon it would be another tree's turn to be admired. It would stand glorious and majestic for one, perfect night.

Jingle Bells

Dashing through the snow,
In a one-horse open sleigh,
O'er the fields we go,
Laughing all the way.
Bells on bob-tail ring,
Making spirits bright,
What fun it is to laugh and sing
A sleighing song tonight!

Jingle bells! Jingle bells!
Jingle all the way!
Oh, what fun it is to ride
In a one-horse open sleigh, oh!
Jingle bells! Jingle bells!
Jingle all the way!
Oh, what fun it is to ride
In a one-horse open sleigh!

Deck the Halls

Deck the halls with boughs of holly,
Fa la la la la, la la la la.
'Tis the season to be jolly,
Fa la la la la, la la la la.
Don we now our gay apparel,
Fa la la, la la la, la la la.
Troll the ancient Yuletide carol,
Fa la la la la, la la la la.

'Twas the night before Christmas,
when all through the house
Not a creature was stirring,
not even a mouse.

The stockings were hung
by the chimney with care,
In hope that St. Nicholas
soon would be there.

The children were nestled all snug in their beds,
While visions of sugarplums danced in their heads.

And Mama in her 'kerchief
and I in my cap,
Had just settled down for a
long winter's nap.

When out on the lawn there
arose such a clatter,
I sprang from my bed to see what
was the matter.

Away to the window
I flew like a flash,
Tore open the shutters and
threw up the sash.

The moon on the breast of
the new-fallen snow
Gave luster of midday to
objects below,

When, what to my wondering eyes should appear,
But a miniature sleigh and eight tiny reindeer.
With a little old driver so lively and quick,
I knew in a moment it must be St. Nick.

More rapid than eagles his coursers they came,
And he whistled and shouted and called
them by name;

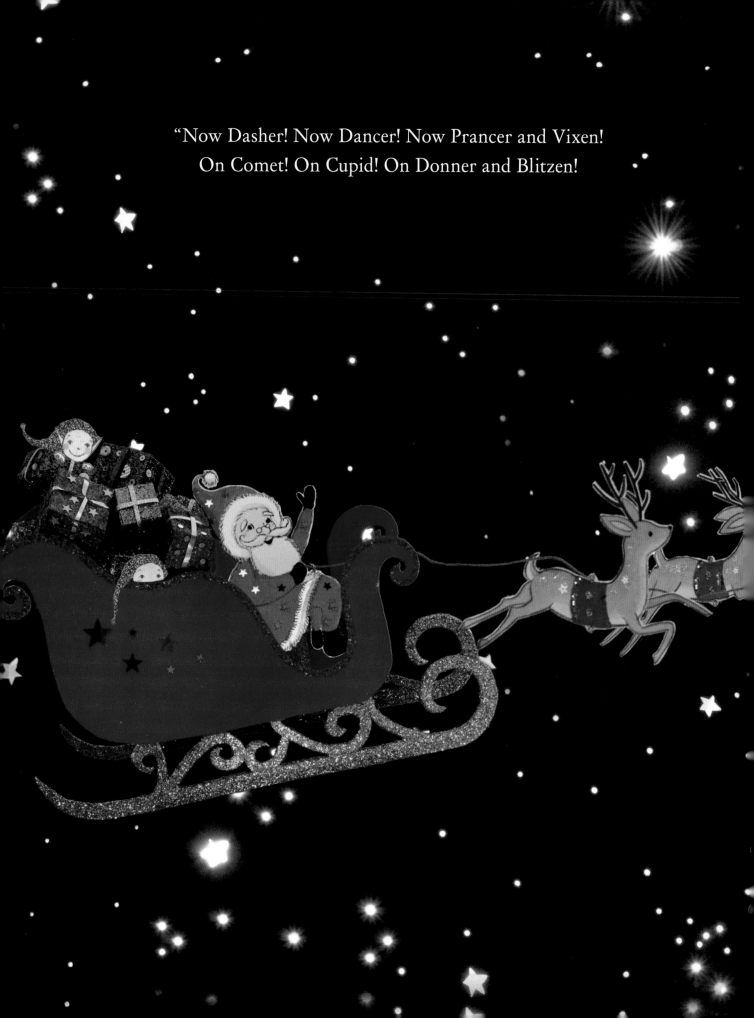

"Now Dasher! Now Dancer! Now Prancer and Vixen!
On Comet! On Cupid! On Donner and Blitzen!

To the top of the porch! To the top of the wall!
Now dash away! Dash away! Dash away all!"

As dry leaves that before
the wild hurricane fly,
When they meet with an obstacle,
mount to the sky,

So up to the housetop
the coursers they flew,
With a sleigh full of toys
and St. Nicholas, too.

And then in a twinkling,
I heard on the roof
The prancing and pawing
of each little hoof.

As I drew in my head,
and was turning around,
Down the chimney St. Nicholas
came with a bound.

He was dressed all in fur,
from his head to his foot,
And his clothes were all tarnished
with ashes and soot.

A bundle of toys he had flung on his back,
And he looked like a pedlar
just opening his pack.

His eyes—how they twinkled!
His dimples—how merry!
His cheeks were like roses, his nose like a cherry!
His droll little mouth was drawn up like a bow,
And the beard of his chin was as white as the snow.

He had a broad face
and a little round belly,
That shook when he laughed,
like a bowlful of jelly.

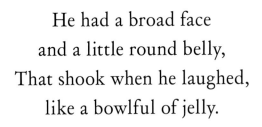

He was chubby and plump,
a right jolly old elf,
And I laughed when I saw him,
in spite of myself.

A wink of his eye
and a twist of his head,
Soon gave me to know
I had nothing to dread.

He spoke not a word,
but went straight to his work,
And filled all the stockings,
then turned with a jerk,

And laying his finger
aside of his nose
And giving a nod,
up the chimney he rose.

He sprang to his sleigh,
to his team gave a whistle,
And away they all flew
like the down of a thistle.

But I heard him exclaim
ere he drove out of sight,

"Merry Christmas to all ...

The First Noel

The first Noel, the angels did say
Was to certain poor shepherds in fields as they lay;
In fields where they lay, keeping their sheep,
On a cold winter's night that was so deep.

Noel, Noel, Noel, Noel
Born is the King of Israel.

Good King Wenceslas

Good King Wenceslas looked out, on the Feast of Stephen,
When the snow lay round about, deep and crisp and even;
Brightly shone the moon that night, tho' the frost was cruel,
When a poor man came in sight, gath'ring winter fuel.

A Letter to Santa

To Santa,
Santa's Grotto,
North Pole

On Christmas Eve, when the snow was all white,
I sat on the floor with a letter to write.
Before I began, I thought what to say
I'd like Santa to leave for me on Christmas Day.

Dear Santa,
(I neatly wrote)
I hope you are well
when you read this note.
I'm sure you have noticed
that I have been good,
just as my mommy
told me I should.
So if it's alright,
for Christmas I'd like—
a book or a train set
or maybe a bike.

Then when I'd finished, I printed my name,
And added kisses again and again.

Across to the fireplace, I boldly went,
And up the chimney my letter was sent.
For that is the place, I'm sure you will know,
That letters to Santa should always go.
Just how they get there, I don't understand,
But that is the way to Santa's cold land.

That winter's night when the world was asleep,
I snuggled in bed—not a sound, not a peep—
Thinking of Santa and the toys he would bring,
And the fun I would have on Christmas morning.
When, all of a sudden, where could I be?
Out in the snow in a strange country!

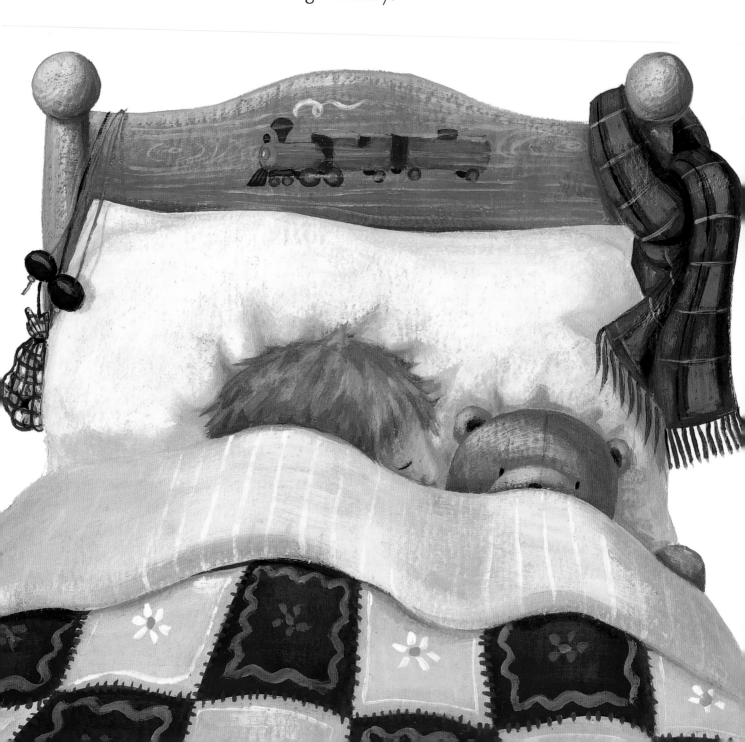

Next to a cabin in the deep crispy snow,
I shiver with cold as I peer in the window.
It's Santa's workshop! I must creep inside.
No one will see me if I'm careful to hide.
Sssh! I must be quiet as I tiptoe in,
To see where our Christmas toys all begin.

Santa's Grotto

141

I can see Santa reading letters galore.
Hey, he's got mine, by his feet on the floor!
A map of the world is pinned to the wall,
Showing Santa the way to the homes of us all,
With rooftop instructions so there is no doubt,
That any small child is ever left out.

Just see how busy all Santa's elves are:
One's making a doll's house, one a toy car;
Another elf's painting a wonderful train,

And this elf is putting the wings on a plane.
Look at that little elf riding a bike,
It's just like the one I said I would like.

This must be the room where presents are packed.
They're measured for size, then carefully wrapped.
Tied up with ribbons and finished with bows,
Each with a name tag so Santa Claus knows.
Wherever you look, there's bustle and scurry.
Everyone seems in a terrible hurry.

Here are the elves who help Santa get dressed.
There's Santa's coat and hat, all neatly pressed.
And there are his boots getting a shine.
They look so smart, I wish they were mine!
I think this room is as good as the rest,
For it's the place that makes Santa look best.

Back in the workshop, the parcel track halts.
It seems there's a problem with one of its bolts!
The elves are worried—there's trouble in the air.
But here comes Santa to make the repair.
In no time at all, parcels speed on their way,
Out to the stables and onto the sleigh.

Outside the stable, the reindeer wait.

I count them all up, and yes, there are eight!

Their hooves are polished, their bells burnished bright,

As elves brush and groom them in the moonlight.

Their harnesses gleam, their coats all shine.

Now the reindeer are restless, since it's almost time!

The sleigh is now packed and the reindeer ready.
Santa at the reins cries, "Away now, go steady!"
High over clouds and hills they fly,
Galloping onward across the sky.
Soon, beneath them, rooftops they see
Where inside asleep are children like me!

When I wake up, it's Christmas Day,
And just like my dream, Santa's been here! Hurray!
My stocking is filled up with candy canes,
And I'm sure in that parcel there must be a train.
Great! There's a bicycle propped by my bed.
My letter to Santa must have been read!

We Three Kings

We three Kings of Orient are,
Bearing gifts we travel afar,
Field and fountain, moor and mountain,
Following yonder star.

O star of wonder, star of night,
Star with royal beauty bright,
Westward leading, still proceeding,
Guide us to thy perfect light.

O Little Town of Bethlehem

O little town of Bethlehem
How still we see thee lie.
Above thy deep and dreamless sleep
The silent stars go by.
Yet in thy dark streets shineth
The everlasting light.
The hopes and fears of all the years
Are met in thee tonight.

On the first day of Christmas,
my true love sent to me
A partridge in a pear tree.

On the second day of Christmas,
  my true love sent to me
Two turtle doves

And a partridge in a pear tree.

On the third day of Christmas,
my true love sent to me
Three French hens,

Two turtle doves,
And a partridge in a pear tree.

On the fourth day of Christmas,
my true love sent to me
Four calling birds,

Three French hens,
Two turtle doves,
And a partridge in a pear tree.

On the fifth day of Christmas,
my true love sent to me

Five golden rings ...

Four calling birds,
Three French hens,
Two turtle doves,
And a partridge in a pear tree.

On the sixth day of Christmas,
my true love sent to me
Six geese a-laying,

174

Five golden rings,
Four calling birds,
Three French hens,
Two turtle doves,
And a partridge in a pear tree.

On the seventh day of Christmas,
my true love sent to me
Seven swans a-swimming,

Six geese a-laying,
Five golden rings,
Four calling birds,
Three French hens,
Two turtle doves,
And a partridge in a pear tree.

On the eighth day of Christmas,
my true love sent to me
Eight maids a-milking,

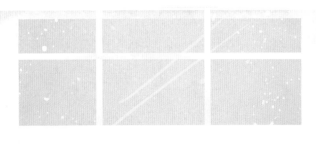

Seven swans a-swimming,
Six geese a-laying,
Five golden rings,
Four calling birds,
Three French hens,
Two turtle doves,
And a partridge in a pear tree.

On the ninth day of Christmas,
my true love sent to me
Nine ladies dancing,

Eight maids a-milking,
Seven swans a-swimming,
Six geese a-laying,
Five golden rings,
Four calling birds,
Three French hens,
Two turtle doves,
And a partridge in a pear tree.

On the tenth day of Christmas,
my true love sent to me
Ten lords a-leaping,

Nine ladies dancing,
Eight maids a-milking,
Seven swans a-swimming,
Six geese a-laying,
Five golden rings,
Four calling birds,
Three French hens,
Two turtle doves,
And a partridge in a pear tree.

On the eleventh day of Christmas,
my true love sent to me
Eleven pipers piping,

Ten lords a-leaping,
Nine ladies dancing,
Eight maids a-milking,
Seven swans a-swimming,
Six geese a-laying,
Five golden rings,
Four calling birds,
Three French hens,
Two turtle doves,
And a partridge in a pear tree.

On the twelfth day of Christmas,
  my true love sent to me
  Twelve drummers drumming,

Eleven pipers piping,
Ten lords a-leaping,
Nine ladies dancing,
Eight maids a-milking,
Seven swans a-swimming,
Six geese a-laying,
Five golden rings,
Four calling birds,
Three French hens,
Two turtle doves,
And a partridge in a pear tree!

Silent Night

Silent night, holy night,
All is calm, all is bright;
Round yon virgin, mother and child,
Holy infant so tender and mild,
Sleep in heavenly peace,
Sleep in heavenly peace.

O Come, All Ye Faithful

O come, all ye faithful,
Joyful and triumphant!
O come ye, O come ye to Bethlehem;

Come and behold him,
Born the King of Angels;
O come, let us adore Him,
O come, let us adore Him,
O come, let us adore Him,
Christ the Lord.